ADVENTURES IN WILD SPACE

THE SNARE

*It is a time of darkness. With the end of
the Clone Wars and the destruction of
the Jedi Order, the evil Emperor
Palpatine rules the galaxy unopposed.*

*As the Empire expands into the unknown
star systems of WILD SPACE, the Imperial
Captain Korda has kidnapped the explorers
Auric and Rhyssa Graf, and hopes to use
their maps and data to his advantage.*

*The Grafs' children, Milo and Lina, narrowly
escaped Korda in their parents' ship, the
WHISPER BIRD, and are now on course to
the planet Thune, looking for help....*

CHAPTER 1
POWER FAILURE

THE *WHISPER BIRD* was in trouble and
Lina Graf knew it. As soon as she'd brought the
ship out of hyperspace it had started jerking
around like a bucking bantha.

"Lina, what are you doing?" her younger
brother Milo complained as he was almost
thrown out of his seat at the rear of the cramped
cockpit.

"Trying to fly straight," she snapped back as
she flicked some switches on the main console.
Warning lights flashed on and off, and no matter
how hard Lina tried, she couldn't get the control
stick to turn.

The ship shook violently, tossing both children around in their seats.

"You call *that* straight?" Milo shouted.

"Master Milo, please!" the droid CR-8R yelled. He was sitting to the right of Lina, linked directly into the navicomputer. "Mistress Lina is trying her best."

"But what if her best isn't good enough?" Milo grumbled under his breath.

"Then you being a backseat pilot isn't helping!" CR-8R shouted.

CR-8R, or Crater to his friends, was a patchwork droid cobbled together by Lina and Milo's mother from a bunch of different parts. He had an astromech's casing as his body, which was connected to a hovering probot base. He had manipulator arms that spun around in the air as he spoke. He was overbearing, argumentative, and very annoying, but right now, he was also all Milo and Lina had.

Their parents were gone. Auric and Rhyssa Graf were explorers who had been mapping the unknown reaches of Wild Space when they were captured by an Imperial Navy officer named Captain Korda. Lina had always believed that the Empire was a force for good that spread peace and order across the galaxy. How wrong could she have been? Korda had stolen their maps, taken their parents, and tried to blow up the *Whisper Bird* with Lina and Milo inside. Now they were alone, with only cranky CR-8R and Morq, Milo's pet Kowakian monkey-lizard, for company. Lina couldn't admit it to her younger brother, but she was terrified. And even though Milo was trying to put on a brave face, she knew he felt the same way.

But for now, they had bigger problems. The *Whisper Bird* had sustained considerable damage when they escaped Korda's explosive blasts. The ship had only just barely held together during the jump to hyperspace.

"We're approaching Thune," CR-8R reported.

Lina glanced up through the cockpit's canopy and spotted a small brown-and-blue planet up ahead of them.

"Are we going to make it?" Milo asked. He hung on to his seat as Morq clung to him, wailing pitifully.

"Of course we are," said Lina. "Just as long as we don't fall apart first."

"And how likely is *that*?" Milo replied.

Just then, there was a sharp crack from above, and sparks exploded from the console's power indicators.

"More likely by the second!" she admitted, waving the smoke away from her face with her hand. "Crater, what's happening?"

The droid consulted the *Whisper Bird*'s fault locators. "Where do you want me to start? Systems are shutting down all over the ship.

The thrusters are overheating and life support systems are in critical condition!"

"What *is* working?" Milo asked.

"The food synthesizer is operational," CR-8R replied dryly.

"Great. Anyone hungry for a snack?" Milo said sarcastically.

Just then, a small explosion echoed through the *Whisper Bird*.

"Never mind," CR-8R reported. "The food synthesizer just blew up!"

Lina wanted to bang her head against the control console.

"We need to make planetfall for repairs," she said, trying to hold herself together.

"Did you have to use the word *fall*?" Milo said.

"Why not?" Lina snapped. "Because if the repulsors give out that's *exactly* what we will be doing!"

"The life support systems are in critical condition," CR-8R repeated.

"Will you just shut up!" Lina shouted.

"Don't blast the messenger," CR-8R snapped. "It's not my fault the ship is falling apart around our audio sensors."

Lina hopped out of the pilot's chair and checked the readouts on the rear console.

"There's the problem," she announced as she brought up a holographic display of the *Whisper Bird's* engines. "The main generator is failing, which is knocking out all the other systems."

"Can you fix it?" Milo asked nervously. His voice shook, betraying how scared he was.

Lina had always been good with machines. When she was little, she had loved taking apart her toys to see how they worked, instead of playing with them. Of course, the *Whisper Bird* was a lot more complex than her childhood toys, but she could do it. She had to. She was the older sibling. With her parents gone, she was in charge now.

Lina gave Milo's shoulder what she hoped

was a comforting squeeze. "If you help me, I can," she said.

Milo grinned and gave Lina a mock salute. "Aye-aye, Captain," he joked.

Lina laughed and turned to the droid. "Crater, you steer the ship," she instructed. "Just keep us moving forward, okay? Toward Thune."

"Forward won't be a problem," CR-8R replied. "If we have to turn in any other direction, *then* we may have a problem."

"You can do it," Lina said encouragingly. She opened the cockpit doors and started running toward the ship's engineering system.

"Oh, you think so? How kind of you to say," CR-8R replied sarcastically as Milo followed his sister, with Morq wrapped around his shoulders. "I mean, I've only been flying starships since, let me see, BEFORE YOU WERE BORN!"

While CR-8R continued to grumble under his breath, Lina reached the main hold, with Milo on her heels. She ran over to a ladder on the far wall and started climbing toward an access hatch on the ceiling.

"I can get into the core through here," she called down to her brother. "Even if I can't get it working correctly again, I can trip the backup generators. They should be able to supply enough power to get us down."

"To get us down *safely*?" Milo shouted up. "You forgot to say safely."

"I can't promise that," she said as she reached the hatch. "But we'll be in one piece. Probably."

"I am not a fan of probably," Milo muttered, prompting a whimper of agreement from Morq. Above them, Lina pressed a control and waited for the hatch to slide open.

But nothing happened.

She pressed it again, but the small door still didn't move. Trying not to panic, she hit the manual override and tried to pull the hatch aside herself.

"What's wrong?" Milo called up.

"It won't budge," she replied through gritted teeth. "The mechanism must be jammed."

"Is there another way in?" Milo asked.

Lina felt her heart sink. "Yeah, there is."

She quickly climbed down the rungs.

"So where is it?" Milo asked. "How do we get in?"

"*We* don't," Lina said. "I do."

Milo looked at his sister, confused. "What do you mean?"

Lina moved over to a computer screen and activated a hologram. It showed a blueprint of the *Whisper Bird*.

"The generator is here," she said, pointing at a flashing red light at the center of the ship. "And the jammed hatch is there."

"Okay, so how do you get past it?" Milo asked.

Lina swallowed nervously. "You use the external hatch, here." She pointed toward a small doorway on top of the ship.

"External, as in *outside*?" Milo replied, stunned.

Lina tried to keep the fear from her voice. "That's right."

"Lina, we're in space," he cried. "You can't go outside the ship while we're in space!"

"What do you think spacesuits are for?" Lina responded. "Besides, if I don't, we'll never land safely."

Before Milo could reply, CR-8R's voice crackled over the comms-system. "*Mistress Lina, whatever you're going to do, may I suggest you do it quickly? The retro-thrusters have failed. We can't slow down.*"

Lina slammed her hand against a nearby comms-unit in frustration. "Change course then. Fly us away from Thune."

"*I can't. The controls aren't responding,*" CR-8R said. "*If we don't change course very soon, I'm afraid the* Whisper Bird *is going to crash directly into the planet....*"

CHAPTER 2
SPACE CRAWL

THUNE WAS GETTING BIGGER by the second.

Milo sat in the pilot's seat with Morq perched behind him. Nervously, Milo glanced over to the screen showing the interior of the *Bird's* rear airlock. Lina was inside, wearing one of the family's bright yellow spacesuits and holding a round helmet beneath her arm.

"Mistress Lina," CR-8R said into the comms-unit. "For the last time, this is a really bad idea."

"It's the only one we have, Crater," Lina reply.

"Let me go out there instead," the droid insisted. "I can fix the power cell."

"*The hatch is too narrow. You'll never make it through,*" Lina said. "*Besides, I need you to steer.*"

"I can steer!" Milo chipped in.

"*Lo-Bro, you crash speeder bikes when they're not even moving!*" Lina replied. "*Trust me, I'm the only one who can do this.*"

Milo usually hated it when Lina used his nickname, Lo-Bro, but he was too worried to care right now. He just wanted his sister to be safe.

Milo watched on the screen as Lina lowered the helmet over her head and locked it into place.

"Very well," CR-8R sighed. "If you're determined to follow this crazy plan . . ."

"*I am,*" Lina replied, her voice trembling slightly.

"Let's run through it one more time," Crater insisted.

"*We can't wait any longer, Crater,*" Lina said.

The droid ignored her. "We'll open the airlock and you'll climb to the top of the *Whisper Bird*. The magna-pads on the palms of your hands and your knees will keep you magnetically attached to the hull."

"*Got it,*" Lina replied.

"Once you've opened the hatch," Crater continued, "don't worry about the main core. That will take too much time."

"*Instead, divert power to the secondary systems,*" Lina said from the airlock. "*The retro-thrusters should unlock and you'll be able to take the ship down.*"

"Only when you're back inside," Milo pointed out.

"*Don't worry, I'm not going to hang out up there,*" Lina said.

"In the meantime, I'm going to try to override the repulsors and stabilize the acceleration compensator," CR-8R said. "Otherwise this is going to be a very bumpy ride."

"*It's going to be okay,*" Lina said, but Milo didn't believe her. None of this was okay at all. He wished he could go in her place, but he knew that wouldn't help. While Lina loved machines, Milo loved nature. He was happiest exploring the swamp and discovering new species, not rerouting power generators.

Some help he was.

"Just be careful, okay, Sis?" he said, trying to sound positive. "Who am I going to annoy if you're not around?"

"You annoy me," CR-8R pointed out, only to be whacked by Morq's tail.

"*Don't worry, Milo,*" Lina said. "*I can do this. Crater, open the airlock.*"

Milo wondered if she was trying to convince him or herself. In the copilot's seat, the droid fussed with some controls before announcing: "Airlock, opening in five, four, three, two . . . ONE!"

Lina held her breath as the air hissed out of the airlock and the large door in front of her started to open, revealing stars as far as the eye could see. Her stomach turned and she almost yelled that it was all a big mistake and she had changed her mind.

The door was wide open now. Only a magnetic field protected her from the vacuum of space. She swallowed hard and pressed a switch on a control panel sewn into her spacesuit's sleeve.

"Turning off airlock artificial gravity now," Lina said.

There was a beep and Lina floated up from the floor. When they were little, their mom used to switch off the artificial gravity in the main hold so Milo and Lina could play in the zero gravity. They would cheer with glee as they swam through the air. Suddenly, it didn't seem so fun anymore.

"Lower the magnetic field," she commanded.

"*Magnetic field deactivated,*" CR-8R responded over the comms. A sudden burst of blue static crackled across the open door, and then there was nothing stopping her from floating out into space.

Lina imagined her mom telling her that she could do this, and she pushed herself forward.

She grabbed the edge of the open door and flipped herself up onto the *Whisper Bird*'s hull.

This was it. She was outside the ship.

Her stomach churned, and she thought for a second that she was going to throw up in her helmet. *Not a good idea, Lina. Not at all.* She tried to remember what CR-8R had recited to her from his large databank of knowledge.

"When performing a spacewalk, focus on the ship, not the stars. Look up and you will be

overwhelmed by the largeness of space. Look down and you will see the hull, which is solid and dependable. Take it one step at time and don't rush. The last thing you want to do is slip and lose your grip."

He was right, that *was* the last thing she wanted to do. For an annoying droid, he made a lot of sense sometimes.

Still clutching the edge of the door, Lina pressed another control on her sleeve. The magna-pads on her knees and gloves activated and her knees stuck to the hull.

"It's working," she said.

"*You're doing great, Sis!*" Milo encouraged her.

"*Yes,*" CR-8R agreed. "*But I for one would appreciate it if you could go a bit faster.*"

"What happened to not rushing?" Lina asked.

"*Sorry, I should have said: 'Don't rush, unless you're about to smash into the side of a planet.'*"

Lina sighed. "Okay, you just concentrate on getting those repulsors operational."

"*What do you think I'm doing?*" was the droid's reply.

Lina didn't answer. Instead she paused for a second to orient herself before she started the long crawl to the top of the ship. The *Whisper Bird's* wings stretched to either side, and she was all too aware of the planet looming in front of them. Thune looked huge now, and she could see tiny dots circling the large sphere. Ships in orbit. Maybe even space stations.

Another wave of nausea swept over her. *Head down,* she thought, *focus on the hull. One step at a time.*

As the ship roared forward, she pulled herself along. The magna-pads clung tightly, releasing as she lifted her hands and knees only to kick back in when she slapped them back down again. She could feel the ship shuddering beneath her touch, the vibrations from the failing engines flowing through her body.

"Almost there," she murmured, looking ahead. But before Milo or CR-8R could reply, the *Whisper Bird* shook violently. She slipped and the magna-pads came loose. All at once, she was falling back into space as the *Bird* shot forward. She screamed, flailing her arms. Her outstretched palm brushed against the metal, skidding across the hull, until the magna-pad stuck. She jolted to a halt, the sudden stop nearly pulling her arm out of its socket.

"*Lina, are you all right?*" Milo called. "*LINA?*"

"I'm fine," she gasped, her heart hammering loudly in her ears. "What was that?"

"*The repulsors have fused,*" CR-8R replied. "*The power cell is about to go critical. You have to move, Mistress Lina. Go!*"

Lina didn't need to be told twice. She hauled herself forward, her eyes on the hatch. Her muscles burned and her head was pounding, but she didn't care. She needed to do this, for all of them.

When she reached the hatch, she found the controls and entered a code on the keypad. The hatch opened and the emergency lighting flashed on and off in the narrow shaft below.

"I'm in," she cheered, looking at the short ladder that led down to the generator.

"That's great, Sis. Hurry though. We've got another problem. Actually, make that two problems."

"What are you talking about?" Lina asked just as she noticed something moving out of the corner of her eye. She looked up to see a pair of starfighters racing after the *Whisper Bird*.

CHAPTER 3
PLANETFALL

"THEY'RE COMING IN FAST," Milo said, checking the rear sensors.

"Too fast!" CR-8R agreed.

"Try being out here with them!" Lina shouted over the comms.

"Get into the engineering section, Sis," Milo suggested. "Perhaps they won't—"

The fighters roared over the top of the *Whisper Bird*, zooming past the ship.

"They're gone," Lina breathed.

Milo sank back into his chair. "I thought they were after us," he said, his voice shaking.

"They're heading toward Thune," CR-8R reported. "As are we, if you haven't remembered!"

"*I'm on it,*" Lina replied. Milo flicked through the internal camera feeds and found her climbing down into the engineering section.

"I see you," Milo said. "How's it looking in there?"

"*Smoky. There's been a fire. Some of the cables must have burnt through,*" Lina said.

Milo watched his sister swing over to an access panel. She pulled it open to find their mom's supply of emergency tools.

"*This shouldn't take me long,*" she promised. Milo hoped she was right. He glanced through the front windows. Thune was massive now and he could make out every ship in its orbit.

"Those are the new-model Imperial ships— TIE fighters," CR-8R reported. "They're docking with that space station."

As if on cue, a red light started flashing urgently on the control console.

"Now what?" Milo asked the droid.

CR-8R checked the readouts. "It's the space station. They want to talk to us."

"Why?" Milo asked.

"Without answering their call, that's difficult to know," CR-8R remarked.

"We'll have to ignore them," Milo said. "How long until we hit the atmosphere."

"Six minutes."

"You're kidding."

"Humor isn't part of my programming."

Milo flicked on the comms. "Did you hear that, Sis?"

"*Loud and clear. The core is in bad shape. The transfer coils are fried, but I should be able to divert power. How's Crater doing with the repulsors?*"

"Poorly," was the droid's too-honest reply. "The safety computer is being stubborn. It won't release the repulsors until there's a stable power source."

Just then, the light on the console began flashing again.

"They really want to talk to us, don't they?" Milo said, staring at the space station.

"They've increased the priority of the signal," CR-8R told him. "If we don't answer, they might send those TIE fighters back to investigate."

"*Just answer the call, Milo!*" Lina snapped over the comms. "*The last thing we need is another flyby!*"

Milo pressed the communication control with a shaking finger. "H-hello, there," he said, dropping his voice in an attempt to sound more like his dad. "How can we be of assistance?"

"This is Imperial Harbor Control. We were about to ask you the same question," a woman replied. *"You are approaching the planet at extreme speed."*

"Roger that, Harbor Control," Milo bluffed even though he had no idea what he was talking about. "We're experiencing a little booster trouble, but will sort it out, er, now-ish."

"Now-ish?" Lina repeated from the engineering section.

Milo glared at her image on the screen.

"Unidentified Mu-class shuttle! Please transmit your identity," the harbor controller requested. Panicking, Milo killed the comms.

"What are you doing?" CR-8R asked.

"We can't tell the Empire who we are," Milo insisted. "They think the *Whisper Bird* was destroyed. If they find out we're alive we'll be arrested like Mom and Dad!"

"So you're just going to ignore them?" the droid replied.

"*That won't work,*" Lina said as she pulled on different cables. "*As soon as we're within range, the* Whisper Bird *will just send our IFF code automatically.*"

"Our what?" Milo asked.

"Identify Friend or Foe," CR-8R explained. "Every ship automatically transmits an ID code by law."

"Lina can just override it, right?" Milo asked.

"*Even if I could, I'm a little busy,*" Lina replied.

A red light flashed on the console.

"They're signaling again," CR-8R reported.

Milo felt like screaming. They couldn't have come this far to be stopped by something as silly as an ID code. Up ahead, the TIE fighters were racing back toward them.

"How are you doing with that power?" he

asked his sister, gripping the arms of the pilot's chair tightly.

"*I just need a few more minutes,*" Lina replied.

"We don't *have* a few minutes. Crater needs to make . . ." He hesitated, unable to find the right words.

"Evasive maneuvers," CR-8R said for him.

"*Not with me next to the generator you don't!*" Lina exclaimed.

The TIE fighters were now so close that Milo could make out the twin muzzles of their laser cannons. "I don't think we're going to have a choice!"

"We're coming within IFF transmission range," CR-8R said.

"Crater, you have to do something," Milo pleaded.

"I'm not sure what I can do," CR-8R began. "Even if overriding the code wasn't illeg—"

Suddenly, the droid froze, his head cocked to one side.

"Crater?" Milo said, shaking the droid gently.

"What's happening?" Lina asked.

"He just . . . stopped working," Milo reported.

"He what?" Lina cried.

CR-8R's head snapped up again and his eyes flashed. One of his probe arms shot out of his body and slammed into the navicomputer. "Overriding codes," he announced.

"But you said that we couldn't—" Milo started.

Before Milo could finish his sentence, CR-8R answered the harbor controller's call. The female voice echoed through the cockpit.

"Starstormer One, *we have received your transmission.*"

Milo stared at CR-8R in amazement. *Starstormer One?* What was *that* about?

"Your IFF checks out. Everything present and correct," the woman said.

Milo stared at the comms-speaker as the TIE fighters sped back to the base. "It is? I mean, it is. Good. So we can proceed to Thune, then . . . please?" Milo said shakily.

"*You still need to reduce speed,*" the harbor controller replied. "*Do you require a tractor beam? We could pull you into the station's hangar.*"

"No!" Milo shouted, a little too quickly, before recovering. "We don't need the tractor beam, we have everything under control."

He switched frequencies to talk to his sister. "Lina, *please* tell me we have everything under control?"

"*Rerouting power . . . now!*" Lina reported.

The *Whisper Bird* shuddered, nearly throwing Milo from the pilot's chair. With a squeal, Morq landed in Milo's lap.

"The repulsors are responding," CR-8R said, seemingly back to normal. "Retro-rockets are firing. Acceleration compensators activated."

"You did it, Sis," Milo shouted. "Now get back to the airlock."

"There's no time for that," CR-8R insisted as the navicomputer beeped wildly. "We're about to enter the planet's atmosphere. Mistress Lina, I'm closing the hatch."

"*What? No!*" Lina cried.

"You will be safe in the engineering shaft while we make planetfall," CR-8R said. "Well, as safe as any of us."

"What is *that* supposed to mean?" Milo hissed.

"Starstormer One, *you are coming in too fast,*" the harbor controller shouted over the comms. "*You are going to crash. Engaging tractor beam.*"

"Crater, do something!" Milo yelled desperately.

"I am," the droid replied. "Firing retro-boosters. Full reverse. Hold on!"

The *Whisper Bird*'s hull blazed red as it plunged into Thune's atmosphere, out of control.

CHAPTER 4
NAZGORIGAN

IT WAS LIKE being in an Utapaun whirlwind. It didn't seem that any harm could come from being thrown around in a confined engineering shaft, but that wasn't the case. Every twist and turn of the ship sent Lina flying through the air, bouncing from wall to wall.

"Milo!" she cried out as she was tossed around. "What's happening?"

There was no reply, not that she would have been able to hear it if there were. The roar of the engines was deafening and if being thrown around wasn't bad enough, the heat coming out of the defective generator was making it difficult to breathe.

Lina was thrown upward toward the closed hatch and slammed into the ceiling. She dropped back down just as a thick cable burst over her head and hot steam sprayed out. For a moment, Lina thought she was going to fly into the hot cloud and be boiled alive in her spacesuit.

Of course! The spacesuit! That was it!

She pressed herself to the wall, slapping her palms against the metal. The magna-pads activated and she clung to the wall. No matter how much the ship moved around, she would remain where she was.

She tried yelling for her brother again, but Milo didn't respond. The engineering shaft shook, but Lina held on. She closed her eyes, trying to shut out the pain in her ears. The heat from the generator was becoming unbearable. She couldn't take much more of this.

Then the floor stopped shaking and the engines settled down to a deep but steady rumble. The temperature was still stifling, but at least she wasn't being thrown around anymore.

"Milo?" she gasped, her throat dry.

There was still no answer. Lina kept the magna-pads on, just in case, but the ship's descent seemed smooth now.

If it was a descent at all. Before the ship had started shaking, Lina had heard the harbor controller mention a tractor beam. Is that what had happened? Were they being pulled into the Imperial space station, helpless and without any way to escape?

There was a sudden thud from below, and Lina jolted forward, jerking her shoulders. She couldn't help crying out. She had hurt her shoulder just before her parents had been taken and it was still sore. It had happened messing around in a swamp with Milo, when their only worry in the world had been getting in trouble with Mom and Dad.

That seemed a lifetime ago now.

Lina released the magna-pads, but waited at the bottom of the shaft. A noise from above made her look up. Someone was walking on the top of the ship, right above her head.

Who was it? She remembered the stormtroopers, with their pristine armor and emotionless masks, who had taken Mom and Dad.

And the blasters. She could definitely remember the blasters.

Lina crouched down, looking out for somewhere to hide. There was nowhere, other than the internal hatch that had jammed earlier, the reason why she'd had to make the space walk in the first place. Yes!

She scrambled to the door, only to find that the controls were still dead. Reaching back, she snatched a fusioncutter from her mom's tool kit with shaking fingers. If she could slice through the door, she might be able to escape into the main hold—if it wasn't crawling with troopers already. It was a chance she'd have to take.

She fired the cutter's energy blade as the hatch opened above her head. Lina looked up, raising her hand to protect her eyes from the sunlight that was spilling down from the opening door. She was too late. A monstrous silhouette loomed across the opening, multiple arms flailing around its body. What *was* it?

"Mistress Lina?" came a familiar voice.

Lina laughed and dropped the fusioncutter.

"Mistress Lina, are you all right?" CR-8R called.

A familiar mop of unruly hair appeared.

"Can you see her?"

"Milo!" she shouted, pulling herself up.

Her brother waved a hand in front of his face. "Man, it's hot in there!"

"Tell me about it," she cried, her voice cracking.

Something furry squealed and jumped into the shaft.

Morq scrambled down toward her, throwing his long monkey-lizard arms around her shoulders when he reached the bottom.

"Yeah, yeah, I'm all right, little fella." She laughed, returning the hug. "It's good to see you, too. What happened up there?"

"Stand back," CR-8R ordered. "I'm sending down a line."

A thin fiber rope dropped down the shaft

and Lina grabbed on to it. She sighed in relief as CR-8R began to pull her up to the open hatch. Her body ached so much that she would never have made it up the ladder again.

At the top, Milo helped Lina onto the hull. Morq hopped over to him and climbed up his shoulders.

"Are you hurt?" the droid asked, worried.

"I'm a little bruised and battered, but I'll be okay. I just need some fresh air," she said, taking off her helmet. As soon as she did, a foul smell hit her. "Ugh! But the air here stinks!"

"Sorry," Milo said. "I should have warned you. This place smells."

Then, without warning, he pulled her into a fierce hug. She held him tight.

"You did it," she said. "You got us down."

"To be honest, Crater did it, not me," Milo said, pulling away.

The droid hovered back a couple of paces. "But I won't be requiring a hug. A simple thank you will suffice."

"But what happened?" Lina asked. "I thought they wanted our identification codes."

"And that's what Crater gave them," Milo said with a grin.

"How?" Lina asked.

"It's as much a mystery to me as it is to you," CR-8R admitted. "I was searching my databank for solutions to our IFF problem and discovered a whole archive of counterfeit registration documents."

"Counterfeit? As in fake?" Lina asked.

"That is what the word means, Mistress Lina," CR-8R replied. "I'm glad to see all those years of school have paid off."

"But how did fake codes get into your database?" Milo asked, confused.

"Well, they certainly weren't there before," the droid said, sounding mortified at the very thought. "I can only guess that they are part of your mother's data package."

That made even less sense. Before being captured, Rhyssa Graf had transmitted some encrypted data files into CR-8R's memory. The droid had been decrypting them ever since. But why did their parents have a large supply of fake IDs?

"Can you tell what else is in the data?" Lina asked.

"I'm still decoding most of it," CR-8R admitted. "It's about twelve percent complete."

"Why is it taking so long?" Milo asked.

"Oh, I'm sorry. I've just been busy trying not to crash into Thune. Remember? When I saved all our lives?" CR-8R scoffed.

Ignoring the droid, Lina turned around to take a look at Thune. The *Whisper Bird* had landed in a busy spaceport. Across the rows of starships was a large town with tall stone buildings.

"Ow!" Lina cried as something stung the back of her neck. She swatted her hand against her skin and pulled away with a squashed bug in her palm.

"Oh, yeah, forgot to mention," Milo said,

waving a buzzing fly away from his face. "There are insects everywhere, here. They're *awesome*! Other than all the biting and the stinging. That's kind of annoying."

"You need some bug spray, yes?" someone called from below. The children looked down to see a large and wrinkled alien bobbing around on a personal hover-saucer a meter from the ground.

"Who's that?" Milo asked.

"Activating lecture mode," CR-8R announced. "It appears to be a Jablogian, a native of Nar Kanji. Observe the blemished red skin, the beady yellow eyes, and the unsightly rolls."

"You might also want to observe the pointed ears," the alien shouted, "that can hear every word that rust bucket of yours is saying! Unsightly rolls indeed!"

"Sorry!" Milo yelled, giving CR-8R a kick. "He didn't mean to offend you."

"I can assure you that I did," the droid

sniffed. "You'll never meet a more dishonest bunch of crooks than the Jablogians."

"What was that?" the alien bellowed.

"He said he's sorry," Lina shouted. "And that he didn't mean it!"

"Well, I never," CR-8R fumed. "I save your lives and *this* is the thanks I get?"

"He's never going to let us forget that, is he?" Milo groaned.

"Just be quiet and take us down to the ground," Lina said, climbing onto CR-8R's hovering base. "I've had enough of being up here, one way or another."

"What do you think I am?" the droid complained. "A glorified elevator? Oh, very well. I suppose you'd better get on, as well, Master Milo, although that fleabag of a monkey-lizard can find his own way down."

In response, Morq jumped onto CR-8R's head. Grumbling, the droid floated them all down to the ground.

"That's better, yes?" the Jablogian said. "No need for all that shouting. Welcome to Thune spaceport."

"Thanks," Milo said. He jumped off CR-8R, only to be attacked by another buzzing insect. "I think."

"Thune is a beautiful place," the alien told them. "Except for all the bugs. It's the canals, you see; the entire place is built on them. There's something in the water that attracts insects."

"*Lots* of insects," Lina groaned, swatting her neck again.

"Which is why you need this," the alien said, pulling out a can of spray. "Nazgorigan's patented bug repellent. Guaranteed to make the little bugs buzz off. How many would you like?"

"Sorry?" Lina asked.

"How many would you like to buy? You won't get far on Thune without one can or seven. Unless you like scratching yourself until you're raw, yes?"

"Okay, we'll take one," Milo said, pulling a credit chip from his pocket. "How much?"

"Four credits each," the alien replied.

"*Four* credits? That's a bit expensive!" Milo said.

"Buy two get one free?" the alien suggested, pulling two more cans from his pack.

An insect landed on Milo's nose. "Fine, we'll take two."

"A pleasure doing business with you," the alien said, handing over the cans and stuffing Milo's credits into a leather purse. "Don't forget, if you need more just call my name and I'll come running."

"Your name?" Lina asked.

"Nazgorigan," the alien said, his lips pulling back into a repulsive yellow-toothed grin. "Like it says on the can. Good-bye."

And with that, Nazgorigan was off, hovering toward more potential customers.

Milo shook the can and sprayed the contents over himself. A moment later, he was choking.

"Yuck!" he gagged. "That's disgusting!"

Lina turned away, trying not to laugh. "You smell worse than usual. And I thought that stuff was supposed to keep the bugs away?"

Sure enough, even more flying insects were swarming around Milo now.

"Give me that," CR-8R said, snatching the can from Milo's hands with his manipulator arm. "I'll just spray a little onto my sensor and . . ."

The droid let out a series of bleeps as he analyzed the sample.

"I thought so," he finally said. "You've just sprayed yourself with stagnant water, probably from the canal system."

"What?!" Milo spluttered. "He tricked me!"

"I told you that Jablogians were dishonest. If I had been allowed to continue, I would have added untrustworthy, unscrupulous, and downright criminal."

Nazgorigan was halfway across the spaceport now, spraying himself with what was obviously a can of real insect repellent!

"We go to all the best places," Milo moaned. He trudged up the *Bird*'s ramp. "I'm going to go shower."

"There's a first time for everything," Lina teased. "And while you do that, I'll try to figure out what we're going to do next. . . ."

CHAPTER 5
THUNE CITY

"I STILL REEK!" Milo complained, drying his hair as he walked into the *Whisper Bird's* hold.

"No comment," his sister replied. She had her head stuck in the workings of a small holo-table.

"What are you doing?" Milo asked.

"Just making a few adjustments. Crater won't let me near the generator again," Lina said. "Says it's too dangerous for a human."

"Quite right," came CR-8R's muffled voice from the engineering section of the ship.

Milo ignored the droid. "So you decided to take out your frustrations on the holo-table?"

Lina replaced the table's access panel. "I'm going to contact Dil and don't want anyone listening. I've rigged the transmitter so the signal can't be traced back to the *Bird*."

"Clever," Milo said.

Lina smirked. "I know I am."

Milo threw his towel onto a nearby seat, where it landed on a sleeping Morq. The monkey-lizard squealed as he woke up.

It had been a long time since the children had seen Dil Pexton. The alien was their mom and dad's agent on Thune, a Sullustan who helped the Grafs sell the holo-maps and data they gathered while exploring Wild Space. He'd been a friend of the family since before Lina and Milo were born. If anyone could help them track down their parents, it was Dil.

"So what are you waiting for, genius?" Milo said. "Give him a call."

Lina punched in a code and transmitted the call, waiting for Dil to respond. Amazingly, the Sullustan answered immediately. A glowing hologram of his face appeared in the air above the table.

"*Lina! Milo!*" the alien shouted, his large black eyes widening. Like all Sullustans, Dil Pexton had a domed head, oversized ears, and thick jowls around his mouth that wobbled when he spoke. "*Thank the Warren Mother that you're both safe. I've been worried sick. Your father hasn't been answering my messages.*"

"Mom and Dad have been taken, Dil," Lina told the hologram. "By the Empire."

"*They've been what?*"

Lina told him everything that had happened, how they'd found their parents' camp deserted and discovered a holo-recording of them being kidnapped.

When she'd finished, Dil frowned. "*This Imperial officer. Was it Captain Korda?*"

The name made Milo shiver. Korda had come to the swamp world they had been exploring, demanding that their mom and dad hand over all their data. He was terrifying, a huge brute of a man with a hideous robotic jaw.

Lina nodded. "But we don't think that Mom gave him everything he wanted. She sent us a batch of encrypted files before she was taken."

"*What kind of files?*" Dil asked.

"We don't know yet, but we're working to decode them," Lina replied.

"*No!*" Dil snapped. "*That could be dangerous.*

Bring them to me. I'll have a look and see what they are."

"What we really want to do is find Mom and Dad," Lina said. "We think they've been taken back to the Core worlds, but can't be sure. Do you think you can find out?"

"That shouldn't be too difficult," Dil considered. *"I know a few people in the Imperial Navy. I could call in some favors. Where are you?"*

"On Thune," Lina replied.

Dil's mouth dropped open. *"You're here? Oh, that's wonderful news. Come and see me, and we'll see what we can do. Here, I'll send you my location."*

The holo-table gave a beep and a map appeared on the small screen set into its surface.

"Got it," Lina told him.

"Good girl. Follow the red dot." The Sullustan sighed. *"I'm really sorry about all this, kids."*

"It's not your fault, Dil," Lina said.

"Yes it is, Lina. I sent the Imperials to see your

parents. *I thought it would be a good deal for them—for all of us. I should have known. There was something about Korda that I didn't like from day one,*" Dil said.

"Can't say I like him too much, either," Milo admitted.

Dil gave them a comforting smile. "*We'll find them, Milo, I promise. Just remember—*"

The hologram fizzed. Dil's face distorted with static.

Lina worked the controls, trying to clear the interference. "Dil? Dil, can you hear me?" she called.

The image of their friend solidified for a second before vanishing. Then the holo-projector cut out.

"What happened?" Milo asked.

Lina checked the controls again. "We lost the signal," she reported. "I'll call him back."

This time there was no response.

"Is there something wrong with the transmitter?" Milo asked.

"Possibly. Crater? Have you done anything to the comms-relay?" Lina called.

The droid hovered down from the engineering hatch. "I don't think so. It's a real mess up there. I'll be able to get the *Whisper Bird* operational again, but it'll take time."

"While you do that, I'll go and see Dil," Milo said. Morq hopped up onto his shoulder.

"You will?" Lina said.

"Well, yeah. You can help Crater," Milo replied.

"I am quite capable of repairing the ship on my own, thank you very much," the droid answered.

"Milo, you can't go on your own," Lina said. "It's not safe."

"I'll be fine," Milo said confidently. "Morq will come with me, won't you, boy?"

The monkey-lizard puffed out his narrow chest, trying to look brave, and nodded.

"No, I'll go instead," Lina insisted.

"Lina!" Milo protested.

"No arguments, Lo-Bro. Until we find Mom and Dad, I need to look after you. They'd never forgive me if something happened to you," she said firmly.

"Nothing's going to happen," Milo argued. "We'll go straight to Dil's office, I promise."

"You're always getting lost," Lina pointed out. "I'm going, and that's that. Crater, you keep making the repairs. I'll talk everything through with Dil and let you know what he says."

Milo crossed his arms. "What about the files?"

"Crater can transmit them later," Lina said.

"I don't think that's a good idea," the droid advised. "They could be intercepted by Imperial agents."

"I'll send for you then," Lina said. "Either way, you're staying here, Milo."

She turned to leave and Morq leapt from Milo's shoulder and landed on Lina's back. She laughed. "You're coming, too, boy?"

The monkey-lizard gave an excited warble.

"Traitor," Milo hissed.

"It's probably because Dil always gives Morq loads of treats," Lina said. The monkey-lizard clicked his beak and chirped happily. "So, does everyone know what they're doing?"

"Yeah," Milo moaned. "Absolutely nothing!"

"Don't worry, Master Milo," CR-8R said. "You can watch me work, if you stay nice and quiet. You might even learn something."

"I doubt it," Milo growled as he watched his sister walk away.

CHAPTER 6
DIL PEXTON

LINA WAS GLAD she had Morq with her
as she walked through Thune City. She had
downloaded Dil's map onto her datapad, but she
was trying not to stare at the display too much.
The last thing she wanted to look like was a
tourist.

Narrow streets ran alongside the foul-smelling
canals and were packed with aliens of all shapes
and sizes. Lina had to weave in and out of the
crowd, navigating around the busy market stalls
and jumping out of the way of the speeder bikes
that zoomed up and down with little regard for
pedestrians.

There was noise everywhere, from the boats that chugged along the canals, adding thick fumes to the already smelly air, to the shuttles that roared overhead. At one point, a trio of TIE fighters had flown low over the imposing buildings. Lina had been convinced that they were searching for her and her brother.

And the whole time, bugs and flies buzzed around her, looking for a tasty snack.

"These things are disgusting," she said, slapping them away. She was surprised when Morq reached into her shoulder bag and pulled out a long silver canister.

"That's Nazgorigan's insect repellent!" she exclaimed, recognizing the tube. "The real one, not the stuff he sold Milo. How did *you* get it?"

Morq tried to look innocent.

"You're such a little thief, Morq." Lina laughed. "Although this time I won't complain."

Taking the canister from the monkey-lizard, Lina gave herself a quick blast of the repellent. The effect was instantaneous and the insects immediately kept their distance.

It wasn't long before they found Dil's address. Like the other buildings along the street, Dil's building was made of a dirty yellow stone, rising three stories into the muggy sky. Lina walked up to the doors and pressed the buzzer. A camera on the porch turned to look at her. There were a series of beeps and the door slid open.

Morq hugged her close as she stepped over the threshold and entered the dirty lobby. Dust motes swirled in what little light squeezed through the narrow windows. The entire place smelled musty and there were patches of moss creeping up the stained walls. Why was Dil working in a dump like this?

A screen in the wall flickered on and Dil's face filled the display. *"Lina, I'm so glad you came,"* he said. *"Take the platform up to the top floor."*

Before she could answer, the picture disappeared again. With Morq whining nervously, Lina stepped onto an elevator. With the sound of grinding gears, they rose steadily up an open shaft. The second floor looked deserted, but light poured out of an open door on the third.

"Don't worry, Morq," Lina said, stepping from the platform and crossing the small landing. "This must be it."

She opened the door and found herself in a large room. The only furniture was a rickety old desk in the corner and two wobbly-looking chairs. An ancient-looking air-conditioning unit in the ceiling didn't help cool the place down.

At least the wooden shutters across the windows kept a little of the street's oppressive heat at bay.

"Hello?" Lina called, creeping into the room. Dil was nowhere to be seen, until a door slid open to her right and the alien bustled in.

"I'm sorry, Lina, I was just dealing with a little business," Dil said.

He rushed over to her and gave her an awkward hug. Morq jumped from her shoulders and scampered over to Dil's table.

"Ah, I know what you want." The alien chuckled, walking toward the eager monkey-lizard. He opened one of the drawers and offered Morq a small bag. "Dried clip beetle?"

Morq snatched the bag from Dil's pudgy hands and crammed a purple-shelled bug into his mouth. His tiny pointed beak crunched the shell. Lina grimaced.

"Oh, they're quite delicious," Dil said,

ushering her toward one of the chairs. "They taste like colo clawfish. You should try one!"

"No, thanks," Lina said, sitting down. "I'm not that hungry."

Dil leaned forward on his desk. "It must be because of all the worry. I'm so sorry about your parents, Lina." He glanced out into the corridor. "Milo's not with you?"

"He's still with Crater," Lina replied. "You know Milo. He gets lost getting out of bed in the morning."

Dil laughed and activated the computer on his desk. "What I don't understand is how you got past the planetary defenses? If they thought the *Whisper Bird* was destroyed—"

"That was Crater. He transmitted a fake ID, overriding the IFF," Lina said.

"But how did he get hold of . . ." Dil's voice trailed off and his eyes widened. "Of course."

"What?" Lina asked, confused.

"A couple of years ago, I did a deal with a Trandoshan smuggler. Your dad was furious, but as payment I received a stash of fake ship IDs. I sent them to Auric, just in case."

"And they were in the data Mom sent to Crater!" Lina realized.

Dil nodded. "If she was about to hand over files to Korda, the last thing she'd want him to find was a bunch of fake IFF codes."

"Crater's search must have activated them," Lina said.

"I told your dad they'd come in handy one day." Dil looked at his computer screen. "Now, I've made some inquiries, but I'm afraid no one's heard anything about your parents."

Lina's shoulders slumped. She had been sure Dil could help. The alien noticed her disappointed expression and tried his best to cheer her up.

"There's no need to look so sad. I've only just started," Dil said reassuringly. "Besides once you give me the rest of those files, I'm sure we'll get somewhere."

Lina narrowed her eyes. "The files? How will they help?"

Dil glanced over at the sliding door before looking back at her. "Let's just say that they're important. Wild Space is becoming desirable property you know." He held out his hand. "Are they on that datapad?"

Lina looked down at the pad in her lap and shook her head. "No, I didn't bring them with me."

"You didn't?" Dil snapped, a little too angrily. "I told you I needed them."

"Crater's still working on them," Lina replied.

"Your droid? What's he got to do with it?" Dil asked angrily.

"I told him to transmit them to you later," Lina said. Dil slammed his fist down on the table, sending Morq jumping onto Lina's legs. Clip beetles scattered all over the floor.

"But that won't work," Dil yelled, his voice suddenly harsh. "I need them NOW."

Sweat had started to run down the alien's jowls.

Morq scampered up onto Lina's shoulder to hide behind her head. "Dil, there's no need to shout," she said. "You're scaring Morq."

The alien punched a control on the desk and a holo-projector activated. "Has Milo got them? Contact him now. Tell him to send them over, or better yet, tell him to come himself."

Lina rose from her chair. "And now you're scaring me. Maybe we should come back later."

Dil stood up, sending his chair crashing into the wall.

"No," he barked. "You need to stay."

Clutching her datapad, Lina backed toward the exit. "Tell you what, you ask around about Mom and Dad, and we'll transmit the files as soon as Crater has finished with them."

"I'm afraid I can't allow that," boomed a deep voice to her right.

Lina spun around to see a man standing in the side door. He wore an olive-green uniform and smirked triumphantly at her from beneath a hat. His grin showed the metal teeth of his robotic jaw.

"Hello, Lina," growled Captain Korda of the Imperial Navy. "How nice to finally make your acquaintance. Your mother has told me so much about you."

Lina stared at Dil in disbelief. "How could you?"

The traitor stared at his desk, shaking his head. "I'm sorry," he muttered weakly. But Lina didn't wait to hear any more. She spun around, ready to run back out into the hallway, but her path was blocked by a pair of stormtroopers. They aimed their blasters right at her, ready to fire.

Morq cried out in panic and leapt from her shoulders. One of the stormtroopers turned and fired. The blaster sounded like thunder in the confines of Dil's office. The bolt hit the floor, but Morq was too fast. He crashed past the blinds, escaping through the open window. The trooper moved to go after him but stopped at the wave of Korda's gloved hand.

"That creature isn't important," the captain drawled. "All I want is the data."

He stalked forward. Lina backed away as he moved closer.

"She hasn't got it," Dil said quickly. "D-don't hurt her."

The captain turned his head to look at the Sullustan. "Hurt her? Why on Coruscant would I do that?"

"I can't believe you would sell us out!" Lina spat at Dil. "We've known you since we were babies."

Dil still didn't meet her gaze. "They threatened me, Lina. I was scared. I've . . . I've done some things in the past that I'm not proud of, before I met your parents. Your mom and dad straightened me out, but—"

"But his past crimes have come back to haunt him," Korda cut in. "It was a simple choice—betray you or spend the rest of his days mining carbonite in a Kalaan prison camp. Don't be too hard on him. He took all of two seconds to decide."

Korda took a step closer and Lina bumped up against the wall. There was nowhere else to go.

The captain loomed over her. "There is nothing to be afraid of. As I told your parents, the Empire wishes to bring peace and order to Wild Space. To do so, we require their maps. It's really quite simple."

"Then why did you arrest them?" Lina blurted out.

Korda's wolfish smile evaporated. "Your mother only gave me part of the data—maps of useless rocks. I thought Pexton might have the rest—how fortunate that you're still alive. I trust you'd like to stay that way."

Behind him, Dil stepped forward.

"Captain, please," Dil begged. "She's just a kid."

Korda silenced the Sullustan with a single glare. "She's a criminal, like yourself."

Lina tried not to cry as Korda raised a gloved hand and lifted her chin so that she looked straight into his icy blue eyes. "Now tell me. Where are those maps?"

CHAPTER 7
AN UNWANTED MESSAGE

LINA HAD TOLD MILO not to leave the ship, so of course he'd done exactly that. He wasn't going to have her boss him around. Yeah, she was older, but only by one year. She wasn't Mom or Dad.

It didn't help that he felt so helpless. When the generator had failed, *Lina* had gone on the space walk. *Lina* had gotten the engines running again. She wouldn't even let him fly the ship.

It was always the same. Milo will mess up. Milo will get hurt.

Well, Milo wasn't listening anymore!

Sitting on the edge of the canal, he pulled on

the string that he'd been dangling over the edge. At the end of the line was an insect trap. It was a jar with a spring-loaded lid. A strange creature was crawling around its rim. It had multicolored wings like a Gorsian dragonfly but the bloated body of a slimy reptile.

"That's it," Milo whispered to the creature. "Go in the jar. Get your sweet treat."

He had spread sugar on the bottom of the jar to see what he could attract and this was the best specimen yet. Of all the bugs that swarmed through Thune's thick air, these were the most fascinating. The warts on their backs pulsated, glowing blue as they buzzed around the murky water.

The inquisitive creature hesitated and then darted inside, crawling into the neck of the jar. With a flick of Milo's wrist, the lid snapped shut and the flying toad-thing was trapped. Milo hauled up his prize, peering through the glass as soon as it was in his hands.

"Oh, you're beautiful." Milo grinned.

The creature flew around the temporary prison, its warts darkening to glow a deep purple. Lina could keep her engines and machines; he'd take living creatures over steel hulls and faulty power cables any day.

Jumping up, he ran back to the spaceport, ducking as a large bug swooped down, narrowly missing his head. It was another of the toad-flies.

Then there was another, and another,

dive-bombing him as he sprinted for the ship. In the jar, the trapped creature croaked, its long tongue darting out to slap the glass.

"Friends of yours?" Milo asked as he reached the *Whisper Bird*, the entry ramp automatically lowering.

Once inside, Milo placed the jar on the specimen scanner in the main hold. Dad used the machine to analyze new discoveries while on expeditions. Milo felt a pang of sadness as he imagined how much Auric Graf would have loved to see this strange bug.

Still, he told himself, working the controls, he'd have something to tell his parents when the *Whisper Bird* finally caught up with them. The scanner hummed, bathing the jar in green light.

"Don't worry, little guy," Milo told the insect. "I'll let you go soon."

A holographic copy of the toad-fly had already appeared next to the jar, mapping every part of the creature's body, from its skeleton to the venom it stored in its cheeks.

Behind Milo, Crater descended from the engineering section. "There you are, Master Milo. I thought Mistress Lina told you not to run off!"

"Mistress Lina says a lot of things," Milo said, eager to show CR-8R what he had found. "Look."

The droid peered into the sample jar. "What a fine specimen!" he exclaimed. "A Thunian wart-hornet."

Milo's heart sank. "You know about them?"

"Oh, yes," the droid replied. "Quite common around these parts—and vicious, too. You're lucky it didn't lick you."

"Lick me?" Milo asked.

"Its tongue is covered in venom. Just one lick and you'll swell up like a balloon. Very nasty."

Milo sighed. "I thought I'd caught something rare."

"I'll tell you all about them later," the droid promised. "Your father conducted a study on them five years ago. In the meantime, have you heard from your sister? I've recalibrated the main generator and run a full diagnosis of the *Whisper Bird*'s systems. Everything is good to go."

"So we can take off again?" Milo asked hopefully.

"As soon as we've heard from Dil Pexton, yes!" the droid replied.

There was a crash from the hallway, and Morq ran in, screeching at the top of his lungs. He leapt into Milo's arms and clung tightly to him.

"Whoa, what's the matter with you?" Milo said.

"What's that obnoxious creature done now?" CR-8R asked. There wasn't a lot of love lost between the droid and the monkey-lizard.

"He's shaking," Milo said, trying to pry Morq from his chest. "What happened? Where's Lina?"

A light started flashing on the holo-table.

"Master Milo," CR-8R said, pointing out the alert.

"That's probably Dil," Milo said, running across the hold to check the readout. The signal was transmitting from Dil's office.

"Let me," CR-8R insisted, making his way over to the table, but Milo wasn't about to be told what to do again. Sitting down before CR-8R could get there, he punched the control to answer the call. The holo-projector whined to life and an image appeared above the surface— but it wasn't Dil Pexton or Lina.

It was Captain Korda.

Morq squealed in fear and climbed the wall to hide in the corner of the ceiling.

"*Milo Graf, I presume,*" the Imperial officer snarled, his dark voice threatening over the comms-line. "*Welcome to Thune.*"

Milo didn't know what to do. Shut off the holo-projector? Run and hide? Instead, he decided to ask the question that screamed through his head.

"What have you done with my sister?" he demanded.

Korda laughed cruelly. "*You're an intelligent boy. I like someone who gets to the point. There's no need to worry. Your sister is quite safe. She reminds me of your mother.*"

With a cry of fury, Milo jumped up and swung his arm at the holographic head. It passed through, distorting the image for a second before Korda's face realigned.

"*You should apply for the Imperial Academy,*" Korda sneered. "*We could put all that energy to good use.*"

"I'll never work for the Empire," Milo spat.

"*Everyone works for the Empire sooner or later. We can discuss your future when we meet. That is, if you want to see Lina again,*" Korda said.

Tears stung Milo's eyes, but he wasn't about to cry in front of Korda. "Of course I do."

Korda's smile fell away. "*Then send me your coordinates. I have to say, I'm impressed. My men haven't been able to break your encrypted holo-channel and Lina isn't saying anything. For now.*"

"I'll come to you," Milo said, trying to sound as calm as possible.

"Master Milo, no—" CR-8R started to say, but he was silenced by a wave of Milo's hand.

"You want the data, don't you?" Milo asked.

Korda nodded. "*Intelligent and insightful.*"

"A public place, then," Milo said. "With no guards. Bring Lina and I'll bring the files."

The captain laughed again. "*I think someone has been watching too many holo-dramas, but if you wish. What about Merchant's Bridge? Do you know it?*"

"I'll find it," Milo said firmly.

"*You have thirty minutes. If you're not there, then your sister will pay the price,*" Korda threatened.

"Don't hurt her!" Milo shouted.

"*I haven't yet, but I can and I will. That's a promise, not a threat. Merchant's Bridge in thirty minutes. Be there.*"

The signal went dead, and Korda's image vanished.

Milo sat down hard and started to cry. With a whimper, Morq crawled down the wall and wrapped his arms around the boy, holding him tight.

"We have to call the authorities and report that dreadful man," CR-8R said.

"I keep telling you—Korda *is* the authorities," Milo sniffed, hugging Morq back.

"Then what?" CR-8R said, exasperated. "We can't face him alone!"

Milo looked at the wart-hornet croaking furiously in the sample jar. "Maybe we won't need to." He wiped his nose against the back of his hand. "Where's this Merchant's Bridge?"

CR-8R hovered over and connected himself to the holo-table. A three-dimensional map of Thune City appeared in the air, and CR-8R zoomed in on a large bridge that spanned the canal. It was covered with market stalls and traders.

"Here it is," the droid said. "It has one of the biggest markets in the city."

"How long will it take us to get there?" Milo asked.

"Only ten minutes or so, but we can't trust Korda," CR-8R said, worried. "His men will already be looking for us."

"They don't know that the *Whisper Bird* survived the explosion on the swamp world," Milo pointed out. "And Lina's obviously not told them anything. According to your fake codes this is *Starstormer One*, remember?"

CR-8R wasn't convinced. "Even so, now that they know you're alive—"

Milo interrupted the anxious droid. "The wart-hornets. They tried to attack me when I trapped this one."

"Well, yes," CR-8R said, confused by the sudden change in subject. "They were probably trying to protect one of their own."

"But how did they know it was in danger?" Milo asked.

"Now really isn't the time for a biology lesson, Master Milo," CR-8R scolded. "Your sister—"

Milo stood up and Morq jumped down onto the seat beside him. "Come on, Crater. You love a lecture. Besides, if we're going to rescue Lina, now is *exactly* the time."

CHAPTER 8
CLEAR THE BRIDGE

MERCHANT'S BRIDGE was as busy as CR-8R had said. Milo stood in the middle, trying not to panic. Aliens streamed past him from every angle, hot and sweaty in the midday sun. The ancient bridge was wide. Stalls ran along every side. The cobbled stones beneath his feet were crumbling, worn down by thousands of feet over the centuries. Beside Milo, CR-8R twitched his manipulator arms nervously.

"This is a bad idea. A very bad idea," the droid remarked.

"Coming to this planet was a bad idea, but I didn't hear you talking about it then!" Milo snapped back. Morq sat shaking on Milo's shoulders, although he jumped off when he spotted a stall selling large orange rakmelons.

Milo turned around in a circle, searching the crowd for any sign of Lina. Then, suddenly, their eyes met. She was farther up the bridge, looking straight at him, her body rigid with fear.

"There she is," Milo shouted, shoving aliens out of the way to get to her. "Lina!"

"Master Milo, wait!" CR-8R called.

The droid tried to stop Milo, but it was no use. CR-8R got stuck behind a large furry alien that looked like a cross between a Hutt and a Wookiee having a bad hair day.

"Excuse me, madam," he implored, but the alien wouldn't budge.

Ahead, the crowds parted enough to show Dil Pexton standing next to Lina, looking miserable. The alien had his hand wrapped around her arm. But, Milo wondered, if Dil was there, where was Korda?

Dil pushed Lina toward Milo and she

wriggled out of his grip, running forward. She grabbed her brother and held him tight. "Don't trust him," she whispered softly into Milo's ear.

"Milo," Dil said, trying to sound jovial. "It's good to see you."

Milo grabbed his sister's hand and glared at the Sullustan. "What have you done?"

Dil's ears flushed pink and he raised his hands. "Look, I didn't have a choice."

"Of course you did," Lina hissed, gripping Milo's hand tighter. "You're Mom and Dad's best friend."

"And I'm trying to help them," Dil insisted.

"By betraying us?" Lina spat.

Dil frowned and his tone hardened. "You kids have no idea what's really going on here. This is real life, not flying around with Mom and Dad having little adventures. These people mean business. If you don't do what they say, they'll kill you, or worse."

"What could be worse?" Milo asked.

"You don't want to know. Korda has enough on me to lock me up forever, but I'm not letting that happen, so be smart. Give me the data and they'll let you go."

Lina laughed. "You don't really believe that, do you?"

"It doesn't matter what I believe, just that you've got the files," Dil replied. "You did bring them, didn't you?"

Milo stuck his chin in the air, hoping that the traitorous alien wouldn't see how scared he was. "No. I didn't bring them."

"You little—" Dil began, grabbing Milo's arm and pulling him close. "Don't you realize what you've done?"

"Let go of me," Milo hissed, trying to pull himself free. Around them, the market-goers ignored the struggle, not wanting any trouble themselves.

"I put my neck on the line for you!" Dil shouted angrily. "Korda wanted to come marching in here with blasters blazing, but I said, 'No, let me go alone. Milo's a smart kid,' I said, 'he won't do anything stupid.'"

"Sorry to disappoint," Milo said.

Dil's grip on his arm tightened. "Where are they? Who's got them?"

"Unhand that boy immediately," someone called from behind the alien. Milo twisted in Dil's clutches to see CR-8R speeding toward them, clearing a path with his manipulator arm.

Dil sighed. "Or what? You'll bore me to death?"

"Or I'll . . ." The droid hesitated, then repeated himself. "Or I'll . . . okay, I don't know exactly what I'll do, but it won't be very nice, I can promise you that."

Dil shook his head. "Pathetic."

But before he could say another word, a man shouted above the loud bustle of the crowd.

"Time's up, Pexton."

Dil spun around. "No!"

"Clear the bridge," the man commanded.

All at once there was the sound of blaster

fire, and bolts of energy shot up into the air. There were screams and cries of panic as the crowd ran for cover. Purchases were thrown to the ground as the mass of aliens almost climbed over each other to get away. The woolly female nearly mowed down CR-8R in her panic. Milo turned to his sister. "Let's go, now!"

"Don't even think it," Dil sneered, pulling a blaster from his belt. He pointed it straight at Milo.

"You wouldn't shoot us," Milo said, although he wasn't so sure that was true.

"Don't make me find out," Dil pleaded.

The bridge was almost deserted now. Milo, Lina, and CR-8R stood in the middle with Pexton. Morq sat on a nearby stall, smothered in rakmelon pulp and spitting out the sticky seeds. It was only when he looked up and realized that everyone had gone that he raced over to the children.

Captain Korda stood on the far end of the bridge, flanked by a line of armed stormtroopers.

A second row of stormtroopers blocked the other exit. There was no escape.

As if to emphasize the point, three TIE fighters screamed past overhead before turning and circling the city.

Korda started walking toward the children, his hands behind his back. Both rows of stormtroopers followed the captain, marching in formation with their blasters at the ready.

Dil shuffled closer to Milo. "Don't argue with him," he whispered. "Whatever he wants, just give it to him, for all our sakes."

"Milo Graf," Korda said as he moved forward. "The intelligent boy with the spirited sister. Oh, they're going to love you two at the Academy. Stormtrooper training, possibly? Maybe even officer potential. Would you like that? A uniform like mine?"

Milo didn't respond. He stood there, clutching his sister's hand.

"Maybe you'll even meet the Emperor himself," Korda continued. "Go all the way to

the top. A clever boy like you. There's nothing you couldn't do. Your sister, too. So sure of herself. So strong-willed. Not many people keep quiet when I'm asking them questions."

He stopped in front of them, the stormtroopers standing behind him.

Milo pretended that he didn't care. He had a question of his own.

"What have you done with our parents?" he said.

Korda flashed a sly smile.

"What have you done with my files?" the captain replied.

"Why should we give them to you?" Milo said.

Korda's smile vanished. "Because if you don't, my men will start shooting. We could begin with your droid?"

The nearest stormtrooper pointed his rifle at CR-8R. The robot gave an electronic wail and raised all six of his arms in defense.

"Wait," Dil said, stepping forward. "If I know Auric and Rhyssa, they've hidden the data on that droid. It doesn't look like much, but they love that old thing."

"Old?" CR-8R bellowed, despite his obvious fear.

"Is that right?" Korda said, turning to Milo and Lina. "Are the files in the droid?"

Neither one of them responded, but their silence didn't faze the Imperial captain.

"Very well," he said. "We'll strip its memory, just in case. Thank you, Pexton. You have done very well." He turned to the stormtrooper. "Arrest him!"

"What?" Dil cried. "You can't! I did what you said! All of it!"

"I can do whatever I want," Korda barked. "Drop your weapon or we'll shoot!"

Dil sighed. For a moment, Milo thought Dil was going to throw his blaster to the ground. Then, with a look of sheer desperation, the Sullustan brought it back up sharply, aiming straight for Korda.

He never took the shot. Rings of blue energy blasted from one of the stormtrooper's rifles, knocking Dil off his feet. He crashed to the ground.

Milo let out a cry. He couldn't help it. He was terrified.

"The alien's stunned," Korda informed them. "Nothing more. A lifetime of mining awaits him. As for you?" Korda glared at them. "This is your last chance. Give me those files! Now!"

Milo swallowed.

"Okay," he said.

"Milo!" Lina said, grabbing his arm. "You can't just hand them over."

"I'm inclined to agree," CR-8R added. "Especially since they're in my head!"

"You're more important, Sis," Milo said, giving Lina a sad smile before turning to Captain Korda. "If he wants the files so badly, he can have them. Crater, transmit now!"

CHAPTER 9
SWARMED

WHAT HAPPENED NEXT was not what Lina expected. Behind them, CR-8R emitted a high-pitched shriek, like nothing she'd ever heard before.

"What's it doing?" Korda snapped, his face contorted with pain.

Lina pressed her hands over her ears, but she still felt like her head was about to explode. The whole time, Milo was grinning at Captain Korda.

The stormtroopers shifted, aiming their weapons at CR-8R, ready to fire.

"No!" Korda shouted. "You'll damage the

files." Then he turned to Milo. "Shoot the boy instead. He's useless to us now."

The stormtroopers turned their blasters toward Milo, but before any of them could fire, another noise spread over the bridge. Louder. Fiercer. The stormtroopers looked up to see a giant cloud swirling down on them from the sky.

But it wasn't a cloud. It was a swarm! Thousands of strange insects were flying in formation, bearing down on Merchant's Bridge. Each was as big as Lina's fist.

"Wart-hornets," Milo shouted above the noise. "Watch out for their tongues! Their saliva is poisonous!"

The swarm dropped down on them. They were surrounded in seconds. The noise was deafening, the sound of frantic croaking drowning out their cries. Milo and Lina held on to each other while stormtroopers fired into the air. The blue bolts of energy briefly illuminated the dark mass that swirled all around.

The wart-hornets reacted angrily. They attacked the stormtroopers, trying to find weak spots in their armor. They bit at the stormtroopers' elbows, under their arms, and behind their knees. Other wart-hornets scurried inside the stormtroopers' helmets. Tongues dripping with venom shot out whenever they met flesh, and the troopers cried out as the poison took hold. Lina saw one pull off his helmet, revealing his red, swollen face. Big mistake. The flying toads were all over him in seconds.

Milo and Lina huddled close to CR-8R. Morq sheltered between them. A wart-hornet buzzed right past Lina's head.

"It worked!" Milo shouted in triumph.

"I don't understand!" Lina cried.

"The wart-hornets send out a warning cry when attacked. Crater has just duplicated it, one hundred times louder than it should be. Every

wart-hornet in an eight kilometer radius came to attack the threat."

"But won't they attack us, too?" Lina pointed out.

"Not as long as we stick close to Crater and he keeps screaming!"

But then CR-8R fell silent.

Milo hit the droid in his metal chest. "What are you doing? Keep screaming!"

CR-8R shook his head frantically and pointed at his head.

"He's burnt out his vocabulator," Lina realized. A wart-hornet zoomed in and flicked its tongue out. It licked her shoulder, leaving a sticky mark on the fabric of her tunic.

"Don't let them touch your skin," Milo yelled.

"How?" Lina screamed. Suddenly, she had an idea. "Wait!"

As CR-8R tried swatting away the flying toads with his manipulator arms, Lina searched through her bag.

"What are you doing?" Milo shouted, ducking to avoid a hornet.

"Finding this," Lina said, pulling a cylindrical tube from her bag.

"Is that—" Milo asked.

"Nazgorigan's *real* insect repellent!" Lina cried triumphantly. She sprayed a cloud of vapor over them, smothering first Milo and then Morq. "It smells almost as bad as the fake one but does the trick."

Sure enough, the wart-hornets backed off, concentrating on the struggling stormtroopers.

"How long will this stuff last?" Milo asked, choking on the spray.

"Don't know," Lina admitted, shaking the can. "Hopefully long enough to get away. What's the plan?"

Milo looked sheepish. "Yeah, the plan. I, um, hadn't quite worked that part out yet. . . ."

"*What?*" Lina cried.

"I got the hornets here, didn't I?" Milo replied.

There was no time to argue. Lina looked around. Covering her face with her hands, she ran through the swarm to the side of the bridge. The wart-hornets parted to let her pass, but a few flew closer than she would have liked. Maybe Nazgorigan's spray wouldn't last that long after all.

She reached the edge and looked down at the canal.

"Come on, you three. This way! Quickly!" she called back to Milo, Morq, and CR-8R.

In the middle of the swarm, Captain Korda crouched down on the cobbled street, his arms wrapped around his head. His face burned and he could only see out of one eye. One of those pesky insects had landed on his cheek. He had swatted it away with a gloved hand, but it was too late. His cheek had started to swell and his eyes had watered.

All around him was chaos. Some of his men fired randomly into the swarm while others fell to the ground in pain. Weak fools. Ever since he'd been a boy, Korda had been blessed with a high tolerance to pain. His tolerance had only increased after he joined the Academy. He wouldn't have survived the Battle of Maraken if it wasn't for that ability. He still wore his replacement jaw as a trophy of that fight. A battle droid had tried to stop him and it paid the price. These children would be no different.

But where were they?

In front of him, a stormtrooper was clutching his helmet, trying to yank it off his swollen head. Korda forced himself up and grabbed the stormtrooper as an unwilling shield. He pushed the trooper into the cloud of creatures, trying to clear a path. Just then, he saw Milo running for the edge of the bridge with the girl behind him.

Surely he wasn't going to . . .

Korda screamed for the boy to stop. But the boy clutched his monkey-lizard to his chest and leapt over the side of the bridge, plunging into the water below. The droid followed, hovering over the railing on its repulsorlift base.

Korda pushed the stormtrooper away. Struggling to see, he snatched his blaster from its holster and aimed at the girl through the cloud of flying creatures. Half blinded as he was by the swarm, his shot slammed into the wall of

the bridge as the girl followed the droid over the edge. Chips of stone flew up from the impact, hitting the girl on the leg. She yelped in pain and tumbled forward.

Swatting the bugs out of his way, Korda ran to the edge and glared over. The girl bobbed in the filthy canal water next to the boy. Korda aimed his blaster, but before he could fire, a wart-hornet dive-bombed his outstretched arm.

It covered his exposed skin with its venom. He cried out, the blaster tumbling into the water below.

Cursing, he spotted Pexton's discarded blaster pistol lying on the ground. It was a cheap SoruSuub model, primitive and short-ranged compared with an Imperial weapon. But it would do the job.

Stumbling against the wall, Korda peered over the edge, but the girl was nowhere to be seen. Had she sunk beneath the surface of the canal?

Then there was the sound of an engine. There! The hovering droid was dragging the girl out of the water and into a small wooden boat that was docked on the other side of the canal. Her brother was already behind the wheel.

"Oh, no, you don't," Korda spat, firing the Sullustan's blaster. The bolt hit the side of the boat, scorching the hull, but the girl was already on board. The boy quickly started the engine and the boat sped forward, just as its owner stepped out of a nearby building, shouting after the young thieves.

Then they were gone, thundering along the canal.

Korda slammed his fist down on the stone wall. They were already out of range of the pathetic blaster.

He looked around with his good eye, ignoring the cries of his men. Now that the droid had stopped making that piercing noise, the swarm seemed to be lifting, not that he cared. It had done its damage.

He couldn't believe it. He'd been tricked by two children.

Cursing himself, Korda ran the length of the bridge. At the end, a civilian hunched over a speeder bike holding a cloak over her head to protect herself from the swarm. He grabbed her shoulder and tossed her aside. Without giving the woman a second thought, he jumped onto the bike's seat and started the engine.

The speeder bike shot into the air, scattering

the remaining wart-hornets. Korda made a hard left, his knee scraping against the road as he turned. Gunning the throttle, the Imperial captain rocketed away from the bridge.

Those children wouldn't escape a second time.

CHAPTER 10
CANAL CHASE

"WATCH OUT!" Lina screamed.

Milo jerked the boat to the right, narrowly avoiding a large barge coming at them from the opposite direction. The Klatooinian crew members shouted curses after them, but that was the least of their worries. He glanced at his sister, who was dripping wet and holding on to her leg. "Did he get you?"

"No," she replied. "Some of the debris from the wall hit my leg, that's all."

CR-8R swung around, a can of bacta-spray in one of his manipulator arms. Lina pushed it away. "Stop, Crater, I'm fine. It didn't even break the . . ."

Her voice trailed off.

"What is it?" Milo asked, turning to look over his shoulder. Lina didn't have to answer. A speeder bike was darting down the path that ran along the left-hand side of the canal, chasing them down.

"Korda!" Milo gasped.

The Imperial captain hunched low over the speeder's handlebars, pushing the bike's engines to the limit to catch up. Even from a distance, Milo could see there was something wrong with his face. The left side was twice the size it should have been; the skin was swollen and bright red. One of the wart-hornets must have gotten him. It didn't seem to be slowing him down though. Didn't this guy *ever* give up?

Morq squealed in alarm, and Milo looked ahead just in time to avoid a collision with a small vessel.

"That was too close," he said. "How far is it to the spaceport?"

Lina pulled out her datapad and activated the map. "I don't know where we are!"

"Neither do I!" Milo cried.

"You found the bridge, didn't you?" Lina pointed out.

"Coming from the opposite direction! You're the one who told us to jump into the boat!" Milo argued.

The datapad beeped as it pinpointed their location. "Left!" Lina shouted. "Turn left."

"When?"

"NOW!"

"A little warning would be good next time," Milo said, pulling their stolen boat into another sharp turn. They lurched to the left, spraying foul-smelling water over unfortunate bystanders on the canal's edge.

There was no time to apologize. Korda had crossed a bridge and was still hot on their trail. He steered the bike with one hand and pulled something from his belt with the other.

"He's got a blaster!" Lina yelled as the officer aimed and fired. The bolt hit the back of their boat, sending wooden splinters flying everywhere.

Milo weaved around the other boats on the canal—or at least, that was his plan. With a sickening crunch, he clipped the side of a barge, nearly throwing CR-8R overboard.

"Are you *trying* to sink us?" Lina shouted. Morq jumped up and grabbed her head, his arms around her eyes.

Another blaster bolt struck the boat, dangerously close to the outboard engine propelling them through the water.

"No, but Korda is," Milo said. "Where do we go now?"

"I can't see!" Lina complained, trying to pry the terrified monkey-lizard off her face.

Milo looked at them. "Morq, get off her. If you need to hug anyone, go hug Crater."

Still unable to speak, the droid couldn't object as Morq sprung from Lina's head to his!

"That's better," Lina said, checking the map. "Take a right, then make an immediate left. Korda will be stuck on the other side of the canal."

"So?" Milo said.

"His speeder won't make it over the water." Lina smiled. "He'll have to go the long way around."

"Okay," Milo replied. "But just remember what you said about me crashing things!"

The boat skidded around a right-hand

corner as Korda's blaster fire hit the water. Then Milo turned the ship left. Both children cried out as the boat nearly capsized before righting itself.

"Is he still there?" Milo asked, keeping his eyes straight ahead.

Lina looked around. There was no sign of Korda's speeder bike.

"He's gone, I think," Lina answered.

"Then let's get back to the *Bird* before he finds us again," Milo suggested.

With Lina reading the directions, Milo did his best to steer the boat. Twice he almost crashed into the canal walls, and he nearly rammed into a barge full of grain. But every near collision took them closer to the spaceport, away from Korda!

Milo grinned behind the wheel. They were going to do this. They were going to get away!

Then he heard a piercing cry that sounded like a screaming animal.

"Oh, no," Lina groaned.

"What?" Milo said, turning to look over his shoulder.

One of the TIE fighters swooped low in the air above them. It matched their speed, dropping down above the canal. It was so close that they could see the dark armor of the pilot through the viewport.

"*Stop the vehicle and surrender!*" the pilot commanded over the fighter's loudspeakers.

"What do we do?" Milo asked.

"We ignore him and keep going," Lina replied.

"Ignore the big ship with the laser cannons?" Milo asked skeptically.

"It's not *that* big," Lina lied.

"Yeah, when you're in a Star Destroyer, not a speedboat!"

He pulled the boat around another corner, with the TIE fighter following close behind.

"*I repeat,*" the pilot boomed. "*Stop or I will shoot!*"

Milo shot Lina a worried glance. "He won't,"

Lina insisted. "You heard Korda on the bridge. They can't risk hitting Crater."

Green energy bolts slammed into the canal on either side of the boat. Large clouds of steam rose into the air as the blaster cannons vaporized the water.

"Want to tell *him* that?" Milo screamed.

Lina pointed up ahead. "Go down there."

Milo's eyes widened when he saw where Lina meant. It was a loading channel for the tall warehouses on either side. And it was a narrow stretch of water, not much wider than the boat!

"I'll never make it," Milo said. "It's coming up too fast!"

"Turn now!" Lina shouted.

"No!" Milo yelled.

The TIE fighter fired again, churning the water. It was trying to scare them into stopping. Instead, Lina leaned forward. She grabbed the steering wheel and yanked it to the right. The boat jack-knifed across the canal and crashed into the loading channel, bouncing off the narrow walls.

Instinctively, the TIE pilot turned to follow them, and he realized his mistake too late. Unable to make it through the gap, the starfighter ran into the warehouse, tearing the solar panels from its sides and exploding into a ball of fire. Burning debris rained down, hissing as it hit the cold water.

Milo grabbed the wheel back from his sister, but the boat stalled, drifting to a halt. "What happened?"

Lina crawled over to the engine. A neat circular hole was burned through the casing. "It's dead. One of Korda's shots must have hit it. The fuel's been leaking out. We're lucky it didn't explode."

"Then what are we going to do? Swim?" Milo asked sarcastically.

Lina turned to CR-8R. "Crater, you'll have to use your repulsors."

The droid shook his head in response.

"Look," she said, shoving the datapad into his face. "We're only a couple of blocks from the spaceport. Point your repulsors over the back of the boat and push us. Come on, Korda could be here any moment!"

The droid shook his head again.

Just then, a gloved hand grabbed the back of the boat!

Lina cried out as the downed TIE fighter

pilot tried to pull himself from the water. The black figure reached out for Lina, her terrified face reflecting in his mask's goggles.

"Crater, stop arguing and do it!" Lina shouted.

As the TIE pilot struggled to haul himself up, the droid threw his base over the stern. Gripping the edge of the boat with his manipulator arms, CR-8R fired his repulsors straight in the TIE fighter pilot's face.

The boat shot forward, faster than before. The pilot lost his grip, flying backward into the water.

Milo turned out of the channel and onto a clear stretch of canal.

"Keep going forward," Lina instructed as she consulted the map. "And then take a right next to that landspeeder dealer."

Milo did what he was told as CR-8R's repulsorlift unit whined in protest. Ahead of them, the buildings on either side of the canal thinned out to reveal a cluster of large ships.

"It's the spaceport!" Lina cheered.

Milo turned to look at her.

"Yeah, and Korda, too."

The captain was standing on a low bridge ahead of them, his blaster aimed in their direction and ready to fire!

CHAPTER 11
BLAST OFF!

"STOP. RIGHT. THERE!" Korda bellowed.

"I don't think so," Milo hissed.

"What are you going to do?" Lina asked.

"This," Milo said as he twisted the steering wheel. "Give us one last boost, Crater!"

The boat rocketed forward, hitting a row of stone steps that led up from the water. They shot into the air, soaring over the bridge and right above Korda. The captain fired his blaster upward. The bolts thudded into the bottom of the boat, bursting through the deck and narrowly missing Lina and Milo—but they had jumped out. Never to float again, the boat crashed into the

canal wall, shattering on the stones. It skidded across the street, demolishing a market stall.

Korda sprinted from the bridge, but by the time he'd reached the ruined stall, the children were gone.

"Quickly!" Lina shouted as they raced through the parked spaceships.

"No kidding," Milo replied, carrying Morq

in his arms. CR-8R followed behind, steam smoking out of his overworked repulsorlift projectors.

The *Whisper Bird* was up ahead. Lina fished out her datapad, hitting the control that would open the loading ramp. Behind them, Korda was catching up, running surprisingly fast for such a large man.

"We'll never make it," Milo gasped. Korda had almost reached them. Ahead, the ramp was down and the *Bird's* newly repaired engines automatically powered up.

Suddenly, a figure appeared in front of them, bobbing about on his floating saucer.

"Hey!" Nazgorigan shouted. "That's the lizard that stole my spray!"

"Sorry, can't stop now!" Lina yelled as they dodged around the angry con artist. Behind them, Korda didn't have time to react and slammed into Nazgorigan, knocking the alien from his saucer. The Imperial officer and the

Jablogian rolled along the ground, a tangle of arms and legs.

It was the chance the children needed. They charged up the ramp. CR-8R brought up the rear as Korda tried to untangle himself from the plump alien.

"How soon can we take off?" Milo asked as they ran into the cockpit. Lina threw herself into the pilot's seat and started flicking switches.

"Already disengaging the landing gear," Lina replied.

CR-8R pulled himself into the copilot's position, linking up to the navicomputer while trying to fix his speakers at the same time.

"Hold on!" Lina cried as she pulled back on the control stick.

***

"Get off me!" Korda snarled, kicking Nazgorigan away. Korda sprang to his feet, but it was too late. The ground vibrated as the *Whisper Bird*'s engines fired, blasting the ship into the sky.

"No!" Korda roared angrily. "Vader will have my head for this!"

He couldn't let the children get away. The captain snatched the communicator from his belt.

"Korda to Harbor Control. Enemy ship on escape vector. Form a blockade!"

"Aren't you forgetting something?" Milo asked as Morq trembled almost as much as the engines.

"What?" Lina snapped.

"The space station that's up there, and all those ships," Milo pointed out. "I bet they don't think we're *Starstormer One* anymore."

Lina jumped out of the pilot's seat. "Then let's find out if they know we're coming. Take the controls!"

Milo blinked. "Me? Really?"

Lina moved to the rear control station. "You managed to steer a boat, Lo-Bro. The *Bird* should be a piece of cake."

Milo froze, overwhelmed. Lina grabbed his hand. "You can do this. You saved me. You saved all of us."

"You sort of helped save yourself," Milo admitted.

"That just means that we're a great team, right?" Lina insisted.

Milo broke into a grin and took his sister's place behind the control stick.

"So what are you planning on doing?" CR-8R said, his voice crackling.

"You've got your vocabulator working," Lina said, accessing the ship's communication array. "Pity."

"Well, excuse me for wondering how we're not going to be blasted into space dust!" the droid complained.

Lina worked the controls as Milo launched them higher into Thune's atmosphere. "Dad used to listen to official channels to pick up tips for new planets to explore. If I can just find the Imperial frequencies . . ."

The computer made an unhelpful sound.

"I can't do it," Lina groaned, trying again. "I thought it would be easy, but—"

"It is if you know how," CR-8R insisted. "Let me do it."

The droid extended another probe into the navicom. "Accessing comms channels."

Voices started to babble over the cockpit speakers, Imperial forces communicating across space.

"*Enemy ship approaching.*"

"*Initiate defence grid gamma.*"

"*Maximum alert. Fighters scramble.*"

"What are we going to do?" Milo asked, looking back at his sister. For once, she didn't have an answer.

"I have an idea," Crater said. "If I track the fleet's communication relays, I can triangulate their positions."

"I have no idea what you just said," Milo admitted, "but it sounded impressive."

"It is," Lina said, realizing what CR-8R was

suggesting. "Crater can work out where the ships are located from their transmissions and find a gap in the blockade big enough for us to fly through! It's genius!"

"I have my moments," CR-8R said, making his calculations as the transmissions kept spilling out of the speakers.

"*Time to intercept. One minute forty-seven.*"

"*Do you have them? Repeat: do you have them?*"

"*. . . remember, you can resist the Empire. For your families, your freedom, your very future . . .*"

"Wait," Milo said. "What was that last one?"

"It doesn't sound like the Empire." Lina checked the transmissions. "It's not even an official Imperial frequency."

"What do you mean?" Milo asked, confused.

"It's—I don't know—*piggybacking* on the official channels," Lina replied uncertainly.

"Like a secret message?" Milo asked.

"Exactly. It's coming from somewhere back in Wild Space," Lina reported.

"But if they're talking about resisting the Empire—" Milo started.

"They might be able to help us," Lina finished. "Crater, can you locate the source of the secret message?"

"I'm trying," the droid replied.

"We won't need anyone's help if we can't get past those ships," Milo reminded them. "Do you have all their positions?"

Lina pressed a button. "Transferring them to the navicomputer now."

The *Whisper Bird* burst out of the clouds and soared up toward open space. Milo looked at the computer readout. Red dots appeared in a grid pattern, each one representing a different ship.

"There's an awful lot of them," he groaned.

"But there's no going back now," Lina said. "We've picked up two fighters."

"Where?" Milo asked.

"Right behind us! Look!" Lina cried.

Milo followed her gaze to the display screen

showing the feed from the *Bird*'s rear sensors. Two TIE fighters had burst through the clouds and were gaining on them with every passing second.

He swallowed hard. "They're really fast, aren't they?"

"I think I've located the source of the transmission," CR-8R reported. "The planet Xirl, near the Kalidorn system."

"That's great, but how do we get away?" Milo said.

Ahead of them, the Imperial ships had formed a blockade. Behind them, the TIE fighters were locking their weapons on to the ship.

This time, there really was no escape.

CHAPTER 12
NOWHERE LEFT TO RUN

ON THE GROUND, Korda ran into his waiting shuttle. The pilot turned to greet him, his mouth dropping open.

"Captain, what happened to your face?" the pilot asked.

"Never mind that," Korda wheezed. He was finding it hard to breathe as wart-hornet venom ravaged his body. "Prepare an emergency takeoff. Get us up to the blockade. Now!"

As the pilot prepared for launch, an alarm sounded from the communication console. Korda's heart was already racing, but his pulse quickened even more when he realized who was trying to contact him.

Dropping into a chair, he accepted the call.

A hologram of an imposing figure wearing a black helmet shimmered into life in front of him.

"Lord Vader," Korda rasped. "How may I be of service?"

"You can tell me that you have those maps," the masked figure rumbled.

Darth Vader only answered to the Emperor himself. He was a formidable force.

"Soon, my lord," Korda replied. "We have formed a blockade, but the children—"

"Children?" Vader snapped. "You're being evaded by *children*?"

"We have them, sir," Korda said. "They won't get away."

"Make sure that they don't," Vader commanded, and the holo-transmission ended.

Korda fell back in his seat. He felt sick to his stomach, and it had nothing to do with the venom running through his system.

Sweating, he looked through the viewport. If this didn't work, he was finished.

"There!" Lina said, pointing at the dots on the screen. "There's a gap."

"Barely," Milo said, although he adjusted the *Bird's* flight pattern toward it just in case. "Even if we could make it through there, the ships will be able to block our path."

Lina thought quickly. "Not if we jump to hyperspace."

"When?" Milo asked.

"Now!" Lina replied.

"But we're still in Thune's atmosphere," Milo protested.

"Mistress Lina," CR-8R chimed in. "As you know, the hyperdrive engines won't fire within the gravitational pull of a planet. The safety protocols will activate."

"Not if we turn them off," Lina pointed out.

CR-8R's head snapped around so fast that Milo thought it might explode. "You can't do that!"

Lina smiled. "Actually, I can. When I got the main generator working, I had to bypass the safety cutouts. We could do the same for the jump to lightspeed, stop the computer switching the engines off. It's simple."

"But highly dangerous!" the droid added.

"Only if we blow up," Lina said.

"Is that possible?" Milo asked.

"Either that or the ship falls apart in hyperspace," CR-8R said.

The two children looked at each other.

"Then we better try it," Milo finally said.

"What?" CR-8R screamed.

Energy bolts screamed past the *Whisper Bird*, centimeters from the ship's hull.

"That was the TIE fighters," Milo said. "They're firing warning shots."

"We have an incoming message," CR-8R reported huffily.

"Let's hear it," Lina said.

Captain Korda's voice wheezed over the speakers. *"There's nowhere left to run! Surrender and I'll let you live!"*

Milo killed the comlink. "Do we trust him?"

"The only person I trust is you," Lina told him.

Morq let out a whine of protest. "And the monkey-lizard."

"How nice," CR-8R said sarcastically.

Milo looked at the approaching blockade of Imperial ships. Freedom lay on the other side, and their parents, somewhere out there.

He took a deep, steadying breath. "We'll only have one chance at this. Let's make it count."

"Are you sure?" Lina asked.

"No!" CR-8R insisted.

"Do it!" Milo said.

Lina went back to the controls. She accessed

the ship's power systems, giving commands that usually the computer would never process. There was a warning beep, and she nodded.

"Done," Lina reported. "We can jump whenever you're ready."

"There's no time like the present," Milo said, grabbing the hyperdrive lever. Before he could change his mind, he pulled it back hard.

The *Whisper Bird* jumped into hyperspace, blasting straight through the blockade. Behind them, the TIE fighter pilots were shocked, crashing straight into the other Imperial ships. They exploded on impact.

In his shuttle, Captain Korda stared at the orange flames. "No!" he screamed.

Against all odds, the Graf children had escaped. But where were they heading?

TO BE CONTINUED IN
STAR WARS
ADVENTURES IN WILD SPACE
Book Two: THE NEST